CLASSIC STARTS™

Rebecca of Sunnybrook Farm

*Retold from the Kate Douglas Wiggin original
by Deanna McFadden*

Illustrated by Jamel Akib

Sterling Publishing Co., Inc.
New York

Library of Congress Cataloging-in-Publication Data

McFadden, Deanna.
  Rebecca of Sunnybrook Farm / retold from the Kate Douglas Wiggin original
by Deanna McFadden ; illustrated by Jamel Akib.
     p. cm.—(Classic starts)
  Summary: An abridged version of Kate Douglas Wiggin's classic story of
talkative, ten-year-old Rebecca's adventures after she leaves her home at
Sunnybrook Farm to go live in town with her spinster aunts, one harsh and
demanding, the other soft and sentimental.
  ISBN-13: 978-1-4027-3693-3
  ISBN-10: 1-4027-3693-2
  [1. Aunts—Fiction. 2. City and town life—New England—Fiction. 3. New
England—Social life and customs—20th century—Fiction.] I. Akib, Jamel, ill.
II. Wiggin, Kate Douglas Smith, 1856–1923. Rebecca of Sunnybrook Farm. III.
Title. IV. Series.

PZ7.M4784548Reb 2007
[Fic]—dc22

                                                              2006014681

                     2 4 6 8 10 9 7 5 3 1

                   Published by Sterling Publishing Co., Inc.
                  387 Park Avenue South, New York, NY 10016
                     Copyright © 2007 by Deanna McFadden
                    Illustrations copyright © 2007 by Jamel Akib
                   c/o Canadian Manda Group, 165 Dufferin Street
                        Toronto, Ontario, Canada M6K 3H6
             Distributed in the United Kingdom by GMC Distribution Services,
            Castle Place, 166 High Street, Lewes, East Sussex, England BN7 1XU
               Distributed in Australia by Capricorn Link (Australia) Pty. Ltd.
                      P.O. Box 704, Windsor, NSW 2756, Australia

              Classic Starts is a trademark of Sterling Publishing Co., Inc.

                     Sterling ISBN-13: 978-1-4027-3693-3
                          ISBN-10: 1-4027-3693-2

           For information about custom editions, special sales, premium and
              corporate purchases, please contact Sterling Special Sales
             Department at 800-805-5489 or specialsales@sterlingpub.com.

CONTENTS

❦

CHAPTER 1

The Riverboro Stagecoach

~☙~

 Mr. Jeremiah Cobb had just picked up the mail in Maplewood. The packages and letters were carefully stored on the back of his old stagecoach. He was about to leave when Mrs. Randall stopped him and asked, "Is this the coach to Riverboro?"

The kind old man smiled and said that yes, it was the coach to Riverboro. Mrs. Randall nodded to a young girl standing beside an old wagon. The girl eagerly ran over to them. Rebecca was eleven years old, but she looked small for her age. Her dark hair was braided, and she wore a straw hat.

"Could you please take Rebecca to my sisters' house in Riverboro?" Mrs. Randall asked. "Do you know Miranda and Jane Sawyer? They live in the old brick house."

Mr. Cobb smiled and said, "Why, I know them as well as I know my own family! I'm Jeremiah Cobb. I live just up the way from your sisters."

"It's a pleasure to meet you, Mr. Cobb."

Mrs. Randall helped Rebecca up and into the coach. Then she paid the fare. Mr. Cobb loaded the girl's trunk safely on the back, beside the mail.

"My sisters are expecting her. I should warn you, she needs to be watched all the time. She loves being around people and does like to talk." Mrs. Randall glanced at her daughter sternly. "She gets too excited sometimes."

Rebecca stuck her head out of the coach's window and said, "Good-bye, Mother. Don't worry. It's not as if I haven't traveled before."

Her mother laughed. "Silly duck," she said.

Mrs. Randall turned to Mr. Cobb and explained, "She spent one night away from home at her cousin's and now she's a world traveler!"

"But it *was* traveling, Mother," Rebecca replied. "I did leave the farm. I did pack a bag. I did take a nightgown!"

Mrs. Randall shook her head and said, "Rebecca! It's not proper to talk about nightgowns in front of Mr. Cobb! Please remember that you are a young lady."

Mr. Cobb smiled, and the stagecoach started on its way. As it left, Rebecca leaned her head even farther out of the window. "I'm sorry, Mother," she yelled. "All I wanted to say was that it *is* a journey when you carry a nightgown!"

With that, the old stagecoach rode off along the dusty road from Maplewood to Riverboro. It was so warm that it felt more like midsummer than mid-May. Mr. Cobb held the reins loosely in his hands, and the horses trotted happily along.

Mrs. Randall watched the coach as it rode away, kicking dust up in its path. The packages and supplies she and Rebecca had bought earlier that day sat on the ground. Mrs. Randall picked them up and put them in the wagon. In the distance, the coach grew smaller and smaller.

My sister Miranda will have her hands full with that girl, she thought. *But living in that house with my sisters will do wonders for Rebecca. She'll have every opportunity to become the best girl she can become. I think a good education will be the making of her.*

CHAPTER 2

We Are Seven

⌒♂

Rebecca's dress was so clean and full of starch that it caused the poor girl to slip and slide all over the stagecoach's leather seat. She was so small that she flew up into the air every time the coach hit a bump. If the wheels fell into a rut, up she went all over again!

After each jolt, Rebecca fixed her hat back on her head and checked on her most precious possession, her pink parasol. When she wasn't being thrown from one side of the seat to the other, she would open up her beaded purse and look lovingly at its contents. The few coins her mother had given her as spending money lay neatly inside.

Mr. Cobb was not used to having passengers. After traveling along the dusty roads for a while, he forgot Rebecca was even there. He also forgot that he was supposed to be keeping an eye on her! Suddenly he heard a small voice above the rattle of the wheels. At first he thought it was a cricket or a bird or a tree toad. The voice called out again and again until he finally turned to look behind him.

Much to his surprise, he saw Rebecca hanging out the window as far as she could safely manage without falling. Her long black braids swung back and forth with the motion of the coach. She was using one hand to hold her hat and the other to poke him with her parasol.

"Mr. Cobb!" she called. "Mr. Cobb!"

The driver slowed down to hear her better.

"Does it cost more to ride up front with you?" she asked. "I'm slipping and sliding an awful fright back here. It's making me black and blue. And I want to see everything better, too!"

Mr. Cobb listened to her carefully and then answered, "No, young miss, it doesn't cost anything more to sit up on the bench with me. Hold on one minute and I'll help you out and up."

Mr. Cobb stopped the carriage and climbed down. Then he lifted Rebecca up to the front to sit beside him. Rebecca sat down very carefully. She didn't want to crease her dress. She placed her parasol gently under the bench. Once she knew it would be safe, she sat up straight and adjusted her white gloves.

"Oh!" she exclaimed, "this is so much better, Mr. Cobb. I felt like a chicken in a coop back there. Do we have a long way to go? Please say yes. Oh, I hope we do."

Mr. Cobb laughed. "We've only just started. We'll be on the road for a few more hours at least."

"Well then, that's going to have to do," Rebecca said with a sigh.

"Young miss, shouldn't you be using that parasol? It's quite sunny out today."

Rebecca moved her dress to make doubly sure the parasol was perfectly safe under the bench. "Oh no, Mr. Cobb. I never put it up when it's sunny out. Why, the pink would fade so very fast. No, I only use it when it's cloudy. But not when there's a chance of rain. Water might ruin it as well."

As the two continued down the road toward Riverboro, Rebecca chatted away to Mr. Cobb about her beloved parasol. As she was speaking to him, Mr. Cobb couldn't help but notice her bright eyes. They lit up her small, plain face like two shining stars.

"Did you notice the pink double ruffle?" she

asked. "Did you see the handle? It's made of ivory. But it's scratched because Fanny chewed it when I wasn't looking. I've been mad at her ever since!"

"Is Fanny your sister?" Mr. Cobb asked.

"One of them," Rebecca replied.

"How many are you?"

"Seven. Hannah is the oldest, then me, then John, Jenny, Mark, Fanny, and Mira."

"That's a big family!" Mr. Cobb exclaimed.

"Far too big. At least, that's what everyone says," Rebecca answered. "I do love them all, but it's so much work. Hannah and I have been taking care of babies for as long as I can remember. But it's finished now and that's a relief. Once we're all grown, we'll have a lovely time."

"All finished?" Mr. Cobb asked. "You mean now that you're going to live with your aunts?"

"No, no," Rebecca answered. "The family is finished. Mother said so and she always keeps her word. There have been no babies since Mira, and she's three. She was born the day Father died."

Mr. Cobb nodded. He didn't know quite what to say.

Rebecca continued. "Aunt Miranda wanted Hannah to come to stay with her and Aunt Jane, but Mother said she couldn't spare her. Hannah's so much better at the chores than I am, so I'm going in her place."

Rebecca chatted on to Mr. Cobb about her life back on Sunnybrook Farm. Everyone knew the place as the Randall Farm, but Rebecca thought *Sunnybrook* was a much prettier name. It made her think of warm summer days, sparkling water, and wonderful fun. Didn't he agree?

"Oh, I should think so, young miss," Mr. Cobb replied. He listened as well as he could, but couldn't help feeling like he was being rushed from mountaintop to mountaintop without a good breath in between.

"I do know the area quite well," Mr. Cobb said,

"but I can't seem to locate your Sunnybrook Farm. Is it near Temperance?"

"No," she said, "it's miles away from there! I guess Temperance is the closest town, though. We took the train there from the farm. Then we slept a night at Cousin Ann's before we borrowed her wagon to come to Maplewood. That's when we met you so I could take the coach."

"That's quite a memory you have, young miss! I guess it ain't no trouble for you to do your lessons now, is it?"

Rebecca laughed and said, "I do love my lessons, and that's the truth. I'll be in school here, too. Mother wants me to be a teacher, but I think I'll be an artist like Miss Ross. She was the art teacher at my last school. Oh, she was such a lovely teacher! She gave me my parasol."

Mr. Cobb looked around and noticed that the sun was high up in the sky. "You'd better have your lunch now. It's about that time."

Rebecca looked at Mr. Cobb intensely for a minute before saying, "My stomach does feel hollow. I was so afraid I'd miss the stagecoach that I didn't have any breakfast. What are you having for lunch?"

"Oh, I don't have anything until I get to Milltown. Then I get a piece of pie and a cup of coffee."

"I wish I could see Milltown!" Rebecca exclaimed. "It's supposed to be even grander than Wareham. Why, I'll bet it's just like Paris. Miss Ross told me all about Paris. You know, that's where my parasol is from. It's also where she found my bead purse." The girl took it out to show Mr. Cobb. "See how it has a lovely snap here?" She opened it up and carefully showed off its contents. "I've got twenty cents for the next three months. It's all the money Mother had to spare. She's given it to me for stamps and for ink. It's for paper, too."

Mr. Cobb thought for a second and then said, "No, Paris isn't all that great. It's the dullest place in the state of Maine."

Rebecca looked at Mr. Cobb curiously for a minute. She didn't know whether or not she should correct him. Then she blurted out, "Oh no, Mr. Cobb. I don't mean *that* Paris. I mean the Paris that's the capital of France. You can't get there by wagon—only by boat. It's the grandest place on Earth—full of beautiful women and lively dancing. I can see it so clearly when I close my eyes."

She squeezed her fiery black eyes shut for effect. "But I'll bet you can see Milltown just as clearly as I can see Paris."

Mr. Cobb laughed. "You know, young miss, if your aunt Miranda will let me, I'll take you to Milltown someday this summer when the stagecoach isn't full."

A thrill of excitement ran through Rebecca's

body. It went from the top of her head right down to the tips of her toes. She grabbed Mr. Cobb's arm, held back tears of joy, and said, "Can it really be true? It's not a dream? Oh, I would *love* to see Milltown, Mr. Cobb. It's my fondest wish!"

The old man's heart swelled with happiness as he looked down at this "young miss." The stagecoach came to the top of a hill and then crossed over a bridge. Mr. Cobb told Rebecca that they were very close to Riverboro. He asked if she was scared.

"I didn't think I would be," Rebecca said. "But now that we're almost there, maybe I am just a bit." She held her hands tightly together in her lap.

"Would you rather we turned around and went home?"

She flashed him a brave look and replied, "I'd never go back. There might be butterflies in my stomach, but I can't turn back now. We're having an adventure. Who knows what we'll see once we get there. Why, there might be ogres and giants under the stairs, but there could be fairies and elves as well. You just never know."

Mr. Cobb laughed at Rebecca's odd way of thinking. "How about we go into town as fast as we can and make a grand entrance? Would that make you feel better?"

The child's face lit up for a minute as she thought about Mr. Cobb's idea. She almost told him to go ahead, but then she changed her mind.

"As much as I would love to go very fast, I almost forgot that my mother put me in the back of the stagecoach. Maybe she'd like me to be there when I get to Aunt Miranda's house. You see, then I could step out of the door like a proper lady. Could you stop and let me change seats?"

Mr. Cobb pulled on the horses' reins, and the coach slowed to a stop. Rebecca waited for him to climb down and walk around to lift her down.

Soon she was in the bumpy back seat with her parasol and bead purse tucked safely beside her.

"We've had a great trip," Mr. Cobb said. "You won't go forgetting about Milltown now, will you?"

"Never! I promise on my honor!" Rebecca swore. "And you won't, either?"

"Cross my heart," Mr. Cobb vowed.

The stagecoach rumbled down the road. Soon it came into town, where the streets were lined with maple trees. Then it turned into the driveway of the old brick house. Rebecca's journey had come to an end.

CHAPTER 3

Rebecca's Family

ᥫᩚ

Aunt Miranda held her sister's letter up to the light. In it she thanked Miranda and Jane for their offer to take in one of her girls. In fact, she said that going to church and school in town would doubtlessly be the "making of Rebecca."

"I don't know if I thought I'd be the making of any child at my age," Miranda said. She refolded the letter and placed it on the kitchen table. "I thought our sister would send Hannah, but it's just like her to send that wild Rebecca instead."

"We talked about how someone else might be

sent if Hannah couldn't be spared at the farm," Jane said.

"I know we did," Miranda grumbled. "But I honestly hoped it wouldn't be Rebecca."

Jane said, "Rebecca was a mite of a thing when we saw her three years ago. That's a long time for change. She's had plenty of time to grow up."

"And to grow worse!" Miranda insisted.

Rebecca's aunts continued to talk about the ups and downs of having her come to live with them. Miranda worried every day about how hard it would be to keep the feisty girl in check.

The aunts spent the day before the coach arrived cleaning the house until it shone. Just as Miranda hung the last dish towel out to dry, she said, "If that Rebecca makes us work this hard while she's here, we might as well give up on ever having a rest!"

"But we had to clean the house anyway, Miranda," Jane said to her from the porch.

"Rebecca or no Rebecca." Her sister came up the steps and sat down on a wooden rocking chair. "And I can't see why you've scrubbed and washed and baked so much for one little girl," Jane continued. "Or why you've bought Watson's store out of their dry goods."

"As long as she's under our roof, she'll be clean, well fed, and properly behaved. That's my promise!" Miranda huffed and puffed for a minute. "She'll also learn to sew, to cook, and to do her chores."

"Well," Jane said, "she might turn out to be a good girl after all, Miranda. We just don't know." The two women went inside to wait for the stagecoach and have some lunch. It was well past the time the coach was due to arrive.

"The coach should by here by now," Miranda complained as she looked up at the tall grandfather clock in the hallway. "I wonder what's keeping them. Not that it matters anyway. I've done all I can. The girl has two towels on the back of her washstand, which is all she needs. I'm just worried because children can be awfully hard on the furniture. We might not even know this house a year from now."

Miranda stood up, walked to the front window, and looked down the dusty street. She paced back and forth and kept checking the clock. Jane watched her sister and thought about how Rebecca must feel. *We're not the easiest people to live with, now, are we? She must be nervous about coming to live here.*

With that thought in mind, Jane went outside to cut some fresh flowers from the garden for Rebecca's room. She also left a red tomato pincushion as a little present.

By the time she got back to the parlor, the coach had rumbled up to the side door of the house. Mr. Cobb helped Rebecca climb out just like a real lady. Rebecca handed her Aunt

Miranda a bunch of faded flowers and smiled politely.

Giving her niece an awkward peck on the cheek, the elderly woman took the flowers and said, "Thank you, but you didn't have to bring flowers. The garden's full of them."

Jane interrupted to give Rebecca a hug and a real kiss on the cheek. Then she said, "Jeremiah, you can put the trunk in the entryway. Thank you."

"Oh, I'll take it right up if you want," Mr. Cobb said.

"No, no." Jane replied. "There's no need to leave the horses. Someone will be along this afternoon. We'll just call them in."

Mr. Cobb nodded and gave Rebecca a big smile. "Well, good-bye then, young miss." He turned to her aunts and said, "Good day, Miranda and Jane. You've got a lively little girl there. I think you'll enjoy her company quite a bit."

Miranda shuddered at the thought of Rebecca being lively. She believed that children should be seen and not heard. "We're not used to much noise," she said coldly. "Good day, Mr. Cobb. Thank you for delivering her safely."

Mr. Cobb nodded politely and climbed back onto the stagecoach.

"Come on now. Let's get you inside," Miranda said. "I'll show you to your room. Shut the mosquito door tight behind you to keep the flies out. It's not the time for them, but you should get in the habit anyway."

Shutting the door was the first of

many rules! Miranda told Rebecca to wipe her feet on the braided rug, and to leave her hat and parasol downstairs.

"But it's my best hat," she said.

"Well then, take it upstairs and put it away in the cupboard. I can't imagine what you were thinking wearing your best hat on the stage-coach," Miranda said.

"It's my only hat," Rebecca replied. "My everyday hat wasn't good enough to bring. My sister Fanny's going to wear it now."

"Fine, take it upstairs. Goodness me. But leave that parasol down here."

"Would you mind if I took it upstairs, too? It would be much safer there."

Miranda frowned. "There aren't any thieves around here. And if there were, I doubt they'd want that parasol, but suit yourself."

The instructions continued all the way up to

Rebecca's room. She was told to always wipe her feet when she came into the house and to always use the back stairs. That way the carpet on the front ones would stay new for longer. As she walked up to her room, she should be careful not to trip on the corner of the stairs. There was a rug in the hallway she needed to watch out for as well.

"Now wash your face and brush out your hair before you come back downstairs. Then we'll get your trunk sorted out and unpacked."

Miranda stopped and looked closely at Rebecca. Why, her dress had buttons down the front! "Isn't your frock on backward?" she asked. "Goodness me, child, why are you wearing your clothes the wrong way?"

Rebecca smiled. "Oh no, Aunt Miranda. With seven children at home, that's a lot of buttons. We'd spend all day doing each other up. This way we can all dress ourselves. You know Mira—she's only three, but she can already do up her own buttons!"

Miranda said nothing as she closed Rebecca's door. She shook her head and went back downstairs, leaving the girl standing in the middle of her room to look around.

The room was neat and tidy with high walls. It faced north, and the window looked out onto the barn. Perhaps it was being in a strange place that made Rebecca tear off her hat and throw it on her dresser. She was so overcome with emotion that she pulled back the covers and flopped down on her new bed, shoes and all. Then Rebecca pulled the covers up and over her. She was hidden from head to toe under a blanket of white sheets and frilly bedspreads.

Miranda came back and looked around at the empty room. She noticed the large lump under the covers at once.

"Rebecca!" she screamed.

A dark, ruffled head and two frightened eyes appeared.

"What are you doing lying in bed with your shoes on in the middle of the day? Messing up your clean sheets! You're going to ruin that bedspread with your dirty feet! Get up this instant!"

"I'm sorry, Aunt Miranda. Something just came over me. I don't know what it was."

"Well," Miranda huffed, "if it ever comes over you again, we'll have to figure out exactly what it is. Put your bed back in order now. Our neighbor is bringing up your trunk and I don't want him seeing your room in this state. The whole town would hear of it!"

CHAPTER 4

Wisdom's Ways

◡∽

Rebecca started school the Monday following her arrival at her aunts' house. The classroom in Riverboro was about a mile away. On her first day, Aunt Miranda borrowed a neighbor's wagon to take her into town. Miranda and Jane introduced Rebecca to Miss Dearborn—her new teacher— and got her sorted out in terms of her books and slate.

After the first morning, Rebecca walked to school with Emma Jane Perkins. She loved that part of the day. When the weather was good and the dew wasn't too heavy on the grass, the girls took a shortcut. They walked through fields of buttercups and dandelions. They passed groves full of wild grass and sweet ferns. The girls played and laughed all the way to school.

At the last fence before the road, the two girls usually met up with various members of the Simpson family. The entire family lived in a black house with a bright red door and a red barn on Blueberry Plains Road. Rebecca liked the Simpsons from the beginning because there were so many of them. Susan Simpson was Rebecca's age, and they became fast friends. The twins, Elijah and Elisha, and their sister Clara Belle also went to school with Rebecca. Last there was Samuel "Seesaw" Simpson, who took quite a shine to Rebecca, much to her dismay! Their big, rambling farm was just like Sunnybrook.

How delicious it all was! Rebecca clasped her grammar and math books tightly to her chest with the joy of knowing her lessons. Her dinner pail swung from her right hand. It was filled with butter crackers, an apple, and a piece of gingerbread. Her voice carried her lessons out to any wild animal that might hear her. She loved every minute of her walk to school.

The little schoolhouse stood on a hill. It had a tall flagpole on the roof and two doors in front. One was for girls and the other was for boys. On one side of the schoolhouse were rolling fields and meadows. On the other side there was a stretch of pine woods with a river sparkling in the distance.

Inside, the room was bare and uncomfortable. The teacher's desk and chair stood on a platform in one corner. There was an old stove that heated the room. The walls held a map of the United States, two blackboards, and work by the students. The bigger desks were at the back of the room. These were for the larger children. The smaller ones were up front, closer to Miss Dearborn.

One warm summer day, Rebecca put up her hand for the third time to ask for a sip of water. Miss Dearborn nodded, but lifted her eyebrows as a warning.

Just as Rebecca put the dipper back into the barrel, she spotted Seesaw Simpson watching her. Seesaw was quite fond of Rebecca. Maybe it was because she never had any trouble making up her mind. Or maybe it was because she was always asking questions. It could even have been her long black braids—so unlike his own blond hair. Rebecca ignored him thoroughly, but he couldn't keep his eyes off her.

So once she had gone up to the water pail, Seesaw's hand went up and he asked to do the same. Miss Dearborn sighed and allowed him to go as well.

"What is the matter with you, Rebecca?" the teacher asked.

"I had salty fish for breakfast, Miss Dearborn," Rebecca answered.

While there was nothing funny about her answer, Rebecca's reply sent the class into giggles. Miss Dearborn didn't like jokes, even if she didn't quite understand how having salty fish made the children laugh.

"I think you'd better stand by the pail for five minutes, Rebecca. That might help you control your thirst."

Rebecca's heart fluttered. She had to stand in the corner by the pail with everyone watching! Without even realizing it, Rebecca's hands flew up and she started back to her seat. "Rebecca! I said stand by the pail. Samuel, how many times have you asked for water today?"

The poor boy stuttered, "This is the f-f-fourth."

"Don't touch that dipper, please. This class has done nothing except drink this morning, which means you aren't studying. I suppose you had salty fish for breakfast, too."

Seesaw didn't quite know what to say. "I had f-f-fish, too, yes, just like R-r-rebecca."

The class erupted in giggles again.

"I thought as much. You may stand beside Rebecca, next to the pail."

Rebecca bowed her head in shame and anger. It was bad enough to be punished for being thirsty, but to have to stand beside Seesaw Simpson, too!

The last lesson for that morning was singing. Miss Dearborn asked Minnie Smellie to pick the song. She chose "Shall We Gather at the River." The chorus rang out as the children sang about a beautiful river. Miss Dearborn looked over at Rebecca. Her face was pale with the exception of her two red cheeks. There were big, wet tears

hanging on the ends of her eyelashes. The hand that held her pocket handkerchief trembled like a leaf.

"You may take your seat now, Rebecca," Miss Dearborn said when they had finished the song. "Samuel, you may stay there. Now, class, I made Rebecca stand in the corner to break up this bad habit of everyone asking for drinks all day long. I know Rebecca is thirsty, but once she gets up it seems that the rest of you want to do so as well."

Rebecca went back to her seat and pulled out her singing book. Miss Dearborn's speech made her feel a bit better. The rest of the day passed without any other trouble. Her classmates were very kind to her all afternoon. Emma Jane gave her a bit of maple sugar from her own lunch, and Alice Robinson gave her a brand-new slate pencil to use.

At the end of the day, Rebecca was left alone with Miss Dearborn for her grammar lesson.

"I am afraid I may have punished you more than I meant," the teacher said kindly.

Miss Dearborn, who was only eighteen, had never come across a child quite like Rebecca.

"I didn't speak out in class." Rebecca's voice trembled. "I don't think I should have gotten in trouble for needing a drink of water."

"But you see, you started all the others. It seems that whatever you do—whether it's laugh, write notes, or ask to leave the room—the rest of the class wants to do so as well. It must be stopped."

"But Samuel Simpson is a copycat!" Rebecca said angrily. "I wouldn't have minded standing in the corner by myself, but I didn't want to stand there with him!"

"I know, and that's why I sent you back to your seat. It's all better now, and tomorrow all will be forgotten. How about we work on our verbs?"

That afternoon, the two parted as friends.

Miss Dearborn tended to Rebecca's wounds with a kiss on her forehead as she left the schoolhouse.

∼♡∽

The schoolhouse on the hill was a welcome place for poor Rebecca. It was a good thing she had school to go to or her first summer in Riverboro would have been very hard to bear. The idea of loving her Aunt Miranda was out of the question, but Rebecca tried very hard to like her.

Rebecca wanted to be a good girl. She was miserable anytime she fell below her own standards. It was very hard for Rebecca to live with her aunt Miranda, eat her bread, study the books she bought, and dislike her all the time. She knew in her heart that it was wrong and mean. As a result, Rebecca often went out of her way to please her difficult aunt.

Needless to say, poor Rebecca irritated her aunt with every breath she drew. She always forgot to use the back stairs. She left the water dipper on the counter instead of returning it to its hook. She sang and whistled while doing her chores. Rebecca reminded her aunt of the girl's father, and Miranda did not have a very high opinion of him.

But what a glimmer of sunshine her aunt Jane was to the girl! Aunt Jane had a quiet voice and understanding eyes. She helped Rebecca settle into the ways of the old brick house. The girl learned them slowly, but the weight of it all made her very tired indeed.

Once school was over for the afternoon, Rebecca would sit beside her aunt Jane in the kitchen and sew. Aunt Miranda worked by the window in the sitting room. Sometimes all three of them would work outside on the porch, where a cool breeze would break through the summer heat.

To Rebecca, sewing lengths of brown gingham was tiresome and slow. But she tried her best
and worked hard. She polished her needles with
her red tomato pincushion until they shone, but
they still always squeaked. She broke her thread
more times than she cared to count, pricked her
fingers often, and dropped her thimble more
than she held on to it.

Aunt Jane was very patient. She helped
Rebecca and was proud to see her sewing slowly
improve.

When the first brown dress was finished,
Rebecca jumped at the chance that she might
have another color for the next one.

"I've bought a whole piece of this brown gingham," Miranda said firmly. "That'll make two
more dresses, with plenty left over for patches,
new sleeves, and to add to the skirts when you
grow."

"I know," Rebecca pleaded, "but Mr. Watson said he'll take back part of it and let us have pink or blue for the same price."

"Did you ask him?" Miranda said sternly.

"Yes ma'am," Rebecca replied timidly.

"Well, that was none of your business."

"I was helping Emma Jane choose aprons. I didn't think you'd mind what color my dresses were. Pink keeps just as clean and nice as brown. Mr. Watson says it'll wash up well without fading, too."

"Mr. Watson's quite an expert on washing then, is he? I don't approve of children wearing bright colors. Isn't that right, Jane?"

Aunt Jane said, "I think it would be all right for Rebecca to have a pink or blue dress. A child gets tired always sewing with one color. Besides, she'll look like an orphan girl always wearing brown."

"The last thing Rebecca needs is a reason to be vain," Miranda said coldly.

"Oh, Miranda, she's young and likes bright colors. I liked them at her age, too."

"You were a fool at her age, Jane," Miranda reminded her sister.

"Yes I was, thank goodness. I only wish I'd known how to take a little of my foolishness along with me, as some folks do, to brighten up my old age."

In the end, Miranda gave in and they exchanged the brown gingham for pink. Rebecca and Jane worked on her pink gingham dress in the evenings. Aunt Jane even showed her how to sew a lovely trim of white linen along the bottom of the skirt.

Rebecca's joy knew no bounds! Her fingers flew along as she sewed. One day as they worked, Rebecca asked, "Can I go and play, Aunt Jane? It's twenty-nine minutes past four and Alice Robinson has been sitting under that tree waiting for me so nicely."

Aunt Jane smiled. "Yes, you may go. You'd better run quickly now. Go behind the barn so you don't distract Miranda. I see Susan Simpson and Emma Jane Perkins waiting for you as well."

Rebecca flew off her chair and gave her aunt a kiss on the cheek. She jumped down off the porch and ran as fast as she could toward her friends. After she met up with Alice under the currant bushes, the two girls gestured madly at Emma Jane to join them. She quickly grabbed Susan and ran over.

The four girls snuck off to their "secret spot." It was a velvety patch of ground in the Sawyer pasture full of small hills and interesting hollows. It was the perfect place to create pretend houses! A group of trees concealed the spot and gave the girls some welcome shade on hot afternoons.

They had stored soap boxes full of their props in the secret spot. There were wee baskets, bits of broken china, and old cups. A group of well-worn dolls often became a cast of characters for romance plays. The girls played out their stories for hours, until it was time for dinner.

"Can't we just play for a few more minutes?" Alice asked.

"I'm afraid not," Rebecca said plainly. "I can't be late getting back for supper. But tomorrow we'll act out the princes in the tower! It's scary, but it's a fun story."

"I don't know that story," Emma Jane said. "What happens to the princes in the tower?"

"You'll have to wait until tomorrow!" Rebecca said. "But we shall have a grand time playing it!"

The girls packed up their games for the day and ran out of the secret spot. They headed home for supper, their heads filled with ideas of princes trapped in towers and all the fun they would have after school this summer.

CHAPTER 5

Friday Fun

〜

Friday afternoons were a special time in the schoolhouse. On that day of the week, the students performed dialogues, recited dramatic pieces, and sang songs. As much as the children loved Fridays, many of them were afraid of having to take their turn at the front of the classroom. They worried about learning the lines and about forgetting them once they stood in front of the class. As with anything that comes with hard work, poor Miss Dearborn often went home with a headache on Fridays!

With Rebecca at school, there was a new excitement about Friday afternoons. She had helped the Simpson twins, Elijah and Elisha, earlier in the summer. They had recited three very funny verses that left the class in giggles. She had also helped poor Susan, who lisped, with a poem about a girl with the same problem. It was very funny, too.

On this particular Friday, Emma Jane and Rebecca were to perform together. Emma Jane was shy by herself, but being with Rebecca at the front of the class always gave her more strength.

Miss Dearborn was so excited about the afternoon's program that she had invited a number of people to watch. The doctor's wife, the minister's wife, two members of the school's committee, and many of the mothers were to come. It was a special afternoon, indeed.

Rebecca and Emma Jane were asked to decorate the two blackboards. Emma Jane drew a wonderful map of North America. Rebecca made a beautiful, fluttering flag in red, white, and blue chalk. Beside her flag she drew a lifelike Christopher Columbus. She used as many colors as Miss Dearborn had in her chalk box.

Miss Dearborn was delighted. "I think we should give Rebecca a good hand-clapping for such a wonderful drawing!"

Everyone clapped loudly. Seesaw Simpson stood up and gave a hearty three cheers.

Rebecca's heart leaped for joy. She even felt

her eyes warm up with tears. She could hardly see on the way back to her seat. It was a dazzling moment for the girl. No one had ever applauded for her before.

The excitement over the pictures continued to grow. Alice Robinson suggested that they all point to Rebecca's picture when they sang "Three Cheers for the Red, White, and Blue." Another girl wanted to fill the classroom with wildflowers for the guests. Seesaw thought it was a good idea for Emma Jane and Rebecca to sign their pictures so everyone would know who had drawn them.

Miss Dearborn let everyone out at a quarter to twelve that morning so that the students who lived nearby could go home and change. Rebecca and Emma Jane were so excited that they ran almost the whole way home.

"Do you think your Aunt Miranda will let you wear your best dress?" Emma Jane asked breathlessly.

"I think I'll ask Aunt Jane," Rebecca replied. "Oh, if only my pink calico were finished. Aunt Jane's still finishing the buttonholes."

"I'm going to ask my mother if she'll let me wear her garnet ring," Emma Jane said. "It will look oh-so-nice flashing in the sun when I point to the flag. Don't wait for me to go back. I may get a ride."

Rebecca said good-bye to Emma Jane and then ran the rest of the way home. She found the side door locked and took the key from under the mat. Her lunch was already on the dining room table. Aunt Jane had left a note saying that she and Miranda had gone to do some shopping in the nearby town of Moderation. Rebecca ate quickly and then flew up the front stairs to her bedroom.

On the bed lay her pink gingham dress! Aunt Jane had finished the buttonholes! Could she—dare she—wear it without asking?

I'll wear it, Rebecca thought. *They're not here to ask and maybe they wouldn't mind one bit. It's only gingham, after all. It wouldn't be so grand if it weren't new or pink or trimmed.*

Rebecca took her hair out of its two braids and combed out the waves. Then she tied it back with a piece of ribbon, changed her shoes, and put on her pretty new dress. On the way out the door, her eyes fell on her beloved pink parasol. It matched her new frock perfectly. The parasol wasn't appropriate for school, but Rebecca thought she would wrap it in paper and just carry it on the walk home.

Rebecca took a good, long look at herself in the mirror downstairs. A vision of loveliness gazed back at her! She had never seen such a pretty dress, nor found an outfit to match her beloved parasol so perfectly. She danced out the side door and raced back to school.

"Rebecca Randall!" Emma Jane exclaimed

when she saw her. "You're as pretty as a picture!"

"Me?" Rebecca laughed. "Nonsense, it's only the pink gingham."

"You're different today, that's for sure! See my garnet ring?" Emma Jane said. She held out her hand. "Mother scrubbed it clean with soap and water. How on Earth did you get your Aunt Miranda to let you wear that brand-new dress?"

"My aunts are in Moderation, so I couldn't ask," Rebecca replied. "Why? Do you think Aunt Miranda would say no?"

"Miss Miranda always says no, doesn't she?" Emma Jane asked.

"Y-yes. But this afternoon is so special— almost like a Sunday school concert."

"That's true," Emma Jane said. "Your name is on the board and you drew that lovely flag."

The bell chimed, telling the two girls it was time to go inside. The rest of the afternoon can only be described as a triumph. No tears were shed. All the lines were remembered. All the parents told Miss Dearborn what a wonderful job she had done with the students. Miss Dearborn told them all that it was Rebecca who had done a wonderful job. She was ready, willing, and never shy. But there wasn't a hint of bossiness, nor was she pushy. She was simply pulled to the center of the stage, where her voice rang out pure and true.

Finally it was all over. Rebecca thought she would never be calm or cool again. Miss Dearborn had given them no homework, and she was even looking forward to her chores. Even the thick rain clouds that hung in the sky did not worry her. She floated on her happiness all the way home. Then she entered the yard and saw her Aunt Miranda standing in the open doorway. At that sight, she came right back down to Earth in a rush.

"You're over an hour late!" Aunt Miranda said angrily to Rebecca. "Why didn't you come straight home from school instead of dancing down the road like that? It's something your silly father would have done. And what on Earth are you doing wearing that new dress without asking first?"

"I wanted to ask if it was all right, but you weren't home," Rebecca tried to explain.

"You did no such thing. You put that dress on because you knew I'd say no if I had been at home," Miranda scolded.

Rebecca replied, "If I'd been *certain* you wouldn't have let me, I wouldn't have worn the dress, Aunt Miranda. But I wasn't sure. And it was such a special afternoon, with our concert and all."

"Harumph!" Miranda said. "You certainly didn't need to show off that silly parasol."

"The parasol was silly," Rebecca confessed. "But it looked so pretty with my dress. Emma Jane and I spoke a dialogue about a city girl and a country girl, and it came to me just as I was leaving that the parasol would be perfect for my city girl. And it was perfect, Aunt Miranda, really. I haven't hurt my dress one mite, I promise."

Aunt Miranda frowned. "You've been crafty and underhanded. Look at all the other things you've done! You went up the front steps to your room. I know because you dropped your handkerchief. Then you left the screen out of your window upstairs and let all the flies in. You left all your lunch dishes on the table. There were crumbs everywhere! And what's worst of all, you left the door unlocked. Anyone could have come into the house!"

Rebecca burst into tears. How could she have been so careless? "Oh, Aunt Miranda, I'm so sorry," she said. "I was late coming home for lunch and wanted to rush back to be on time for our concert."

"There's no use crying now. An ounce of good behavior is worth a pound of being sorry afterward. Now take off that dress so I can make sure you haven't ruined it. I have no patience for you acting in your father's silly little ways."

Rebecca lifted her head in a flash of anger. "Look here, Aunt Miranda. I'll be as good as I know how to be. I'll remember to lock the door and won't wear my dress without asking again. But my father wasn't silly. He was a p-perfectly lovely father and it's mean to say such things!"

"Don't you dare talk back to me that way, Rebecca!" Miranda said sternly. "Upstairs to your room this instant. Your father was a vain and foolish man. You might as well hear that from me. It's right to bed for you. We've already put your supper up on your dresser. I don't want to hear another peep from you."

Rebecca wiped away her tears and climbed the stairs with a heavy heart. The wonder and excitement of the day were fading as fast as the rainstorm that was about to drench the old brick house was approaching.

Just then, Jane came into the room. "Why don't you run out and take the laundry from the line," Miranda said. "It looks like we're in for a storm."

"I think we've already had it," Jane said quietly. "I don't often speak up, Miranda, but I don't think you should have said those things about Rebecca's father."

"Think what you'd like, Jane, but the truth needs telling. That girl will never amount to a hill of beans until she stops taking after her father so much. I'm glad I said what I did."

"Well, I'm sure you are glad. But that doesn't change how hurt her feelings were. It simply wasn't nice of you."

A giant clap of thunder shook the old brick house. It might have scared Miranda if she wasn't already thinking hard about what Jane had just said.

Meanwhile, a weary Rebecca closed the door

to her room. She took off her beloved pink gingham with trembling fingers. Her cotton handkerchief was rolled into a hard ball. She unrolled it
and wiped away her tears. Then she braided her
hair back into pigtails and took off her good shoes.

With her wonderful day in ruins, Rebecca
thought about going back to Sunnybrook Farm.
Her mother would be very angry with her, but at
least Aunt Miranda could have Hannah come to
stay. She sat down hard on the chair in front of the
window and thought about everything that had
happened.

What a golden morning it had been! A few
hours ago, Rebecca had sat there looking out at
her bright world. Then there was all the excitement of the concert at school and her wonderful
picture on the blackboard. She had never been so
well liked before.

Rebecca thought, *I'll go to Maplewood on the next
stagecoach with Mr. Cobb.* Indeed, she would slip

away now and spend the night with the Cobbs. Then she could leave with Uncle Jeremiah in the morning.

Once she had made up her mind, Rebecca never stopped to think about her actions. Within minutes, she had on her old brown dress, hat, and jacket. She scrambled out the window onto the roof. Luckily, it wasn't very high up. She grabbed hold of the lightning rod and slid down onto the porch. The rain was falling hard, but Rebecca didn't notice. She ran down the road to the Cobbs' house as fast as she could.

CHAPTER 6

Rebecca Almost Runs Away

Jeremiah Cobb sat at the table by himself. Mrs. Cobb had gone to help a sick neighbor and left him on his own for dinner. It was still raining. The sky was very dark, even if it was just five o'clock. Looking up from his supper, Mr. Cobb was surprised to see a wet, sad little girl standing at the door. Rebecca's face was swollen from crying.

"Mr. Cobb," she said, "may I please c-c-come in?"

His heart went out to her. "Rebecca!" he said, "why, you're as wet as a washcloth! Come right in here and sit by the fire to warm up."

"I've run away from the old brick house!" Rebecca blurted out. "I want to go back to Sunnybrook Farm. Will you keep me tonight and take me to Maplewood tomorrow on the coach? I haven't got any money for the fare, but I promise I'll get it to you."

"We won't quarrel about money, you and me. And we never had our ride together anyway."

"I shall never see Milltown now!" Rebecca sobbed.

"What's happened, young miss?" Mr. Cobb asked kindly.

Rebecca took a deep breath and told him the story from beginning to end. Mr. Cobb listened patiently and did not interrupt her—not even once. When she was done, he said, "Poor little soul!"

"You will take me to Maplewood, won't you, Mr. Cobb?" she asked.

"Don't you fret one minute. We'll figure something out." He got up from the table and poured her a cup of hot tea. The two sat for a minute as Mr. Cobb thought about what he should do. It wasn't an easy decision. There was no doubt that Rebecca's aunts would be worried about her. At the same time, he didn't want to upset the girl. In the end, he made no decision at all—he simply left it up to chance.

"I suppose your mother would be happy to have you home," he said.

A tiny bit of fear crept up and into Rebecca's mind. It grew larger the more she thought about what Mr. Cobb had just said.

"She won't like it that I ran away, I suppose. She'll be sorry that I upset my Aunt Miranda. But I'll try to make her understand."

"I guess she sent you down here with a mind for schooling. I suppose you'll have to go all the way to that school in Temperance now."

"There are only two months of school in Temperance and the farm's too far from any other schools," Rebecca said sadly.

"Oh well!" Mr. Cobb said. "There are other things in the world besides school."

Rebecca sniffed loudly as she took a sip of her tea. "Y-yes, but mother thought it would be the making of me to go to school and to live with Aunt Miranda. But I've failed terribly. No matter how hard I try, Aunt Miranda still finds faults with me. But sometimes I just don't think, either!"

"It'll be nice to be back at the farm with all your brothers and sisters, anyway," he said kindly.

"It's too full. That's the trouble. Hannah's going to have to come to the brick house in my place."

"Do you suppose Miranda and Jane will have her? I should be most afraid they might not. They'll be right upset about you going back home. You can hardly blame them." He looked closely at his little friend for a minute. "How do you like the school here?"

This brought a smile to Rebecca's face. She started to tell him all about her wonderful afternoon, about how much she liked Miss Dearborn, and about the new things she was learning.

"It would be a shame to leave all that on account of one little fight with your Aunt Miranda. She's a sour one, that's for sure, but surely you can be a bit more patient?"

"I guess I could try," Rebecca admitted softly.

"Your Aunt Jane would be right sad to see you go, too, wouldn't she?"

Rebecca nodded. The two sat in silence for a minute until the rain stopped. She finished her cup of tea and looked out at the sun breaking through the clouds.

"I'm not going to go to Maplewood," Rebecca said. "I don't know if Aunt Miranda will have me back now that I've run away, but I've got to face her anyway. Would you be so kind as to drive me back?"

"Your Uncle Jeremiah would be happy to take you back. How about I bring up the load of wood I need to deliver? That way you can sneak back into the house without them knowing. Once you've had a good night's sleep, you can tell them what happened."

And that's exactly what they did. As Rebecca quietly crept back into the house, she felt almost peaceful. Mr. Cobb had saved her from error and foolishness. She was more determined than ever to win Aunt Miranda's approval. She would be the best girl she knew how to be, and she'd make a good go of life in the old brick house.

CHAPTER 7

Rebecca Gets to Visit Milltown

The morning after Rebecca almost ran away, she told her Aunt Miranda the truth. Her aunt was very angry with her, but she did forgive her. She even allowed Rebecca to go to Milltown on the next school holiday.

Rebecca's visit to Milltown was everything she hoped for and more. Mr. Cobb offered to take both Rebecca and Emma Jane, so the girl would have someone her own age to talk to and to play with. It would be impossible for two girls to see more, eat more, or ask more questions than Rebecca and Emma Jane did that day.

Mr. and Mrs. Cobb took the two girls into town on a Wednesday. They had a splendid day. First they watched a play based on *Uncle Tom's Cabin* and then they ate ice cream. In the afternoon, they went to the Agricultural Fair.

The Milltown trip was not without its small tragedies, though. The next week, one of Miranda's friends told her that she'd better keep an eye on Rebecca. Apparently she had been acting quite strangely. Miranda's friend had overheard her saying something dreadful in front of Emma Jane and Susan Simpson. Then she saw the two girls get down on all fours and chase Rebecca!

At first Rebecca had no idea what she had done.

Aunt Jane kindly asked her to try to remember the past few days. "Think very hard," she insisted. "When did they chase you up the road and what were you doing?"

A sudden light broke over Rebecca's face.

"Oh! I see now," she said. "Emma Jane and I were walking along the road. We had just seen *Uncle Tom's Cabin* in Milltown, so it was fresh in my mind. All I did was act out one of the scenes from the play. I must have said the lines out loud, too, and that's what Aunt Miranda's friend overheard."

Miranda squeezed her lips together very tightly. "Well, you've got no call to be playacting in the middle of the street," she said. "But I'm thankful it's not worse. You are born to trouble as fire sparks float upward, young lady."

Rebecca wanted to say something further, but she held her tongue. She was keeping her promise of trying to fit in at the brick house—even if she did think Aunt Miranda was unfair to misjudge their playacting for something else.

"Now run off and lay the plates for dinner," Miranda said.

Rebecca did exactly as she was told. Her heavy feet carried her into the kitchen to set the table. Miranda turned to Jane and said, "I declare, she is the strangest child!" She put her mending down on her lap. "You don't think she's a mite bit crazy?"

"I don't think she's much like the rest of us," Jane said. "But she's got it in her to be whatever she wants to be when she grows up. I guess we'll just have to wait and see what she becomes."

CHAPTER 8

Daydreams Lead to Trouble

⟡

Rebecca worked very hard both at home and in school. Slowly her Aunt Miranda began to see improvements. After that fateful day when she almost ran away, Rebecca never forgot to close the screen door and always remembered to go up the back stairs. As a reward for being such a good girl, Aunt Miranda gave Rebecca permission to visit with the Cobbs.

Dressed in her very best, Rebecca made her way to the Cobbs' house to have tea with them. As she was crossing the bridge, she was suddenly struck by the beauty of the river. She leaned well over the new railing to look at the water splashing down the falls. Resting her elbows on the wooden slat, she stood there daydreaming.

Suddenly a strange smell caught her nose.

"Why, it's paint!" she cried. "And it's all over my best dress! What *will* Aunt Miranda say!"

With tears running down her face, Rebecca ran to the Cobbs. She hoped they could help her.

Mrs. Cobb took one look at the dress and said, "Don't you worry, I'm sure I can get those stains out!"

She handed Rebecca an old blue calico housedress to wear in the meantime. They started by soaking the dress in turpentine. "If this doesn't work," Mrs. Cobb said, "we can always try chalk. It works well on stains."

Rebecca's face was so sad. "Do you think we can save the dress? Aunt Miranda is going to be so angry with me."

Mrs. Cobb replied, "Yes, I do. Even if the chalk doesn't work, we can still try scrubbing it hard with the suds." She put a hand on Rebecca's shoulder and squeezed. "Now, don't let this ruin your appetite. I've got some good cream biscuit and honey for you. Go on and sit down at the table."

She sat down beside Mr. Cobb, who handed her a plate with biscuits.

"There's just one thing I don't understand," Mr. Cobb said plainly. "How'd you get it all over yourself? There are signs all over the bridge telling people about the wet paint."

"I didn't notice any signs," Rebecca said with a sigh. "I was looking at the falls and daydreaming about my new poem."

After supper, Rebecca insisted on doing the dishes as Mrs. Cobb tried to get the paint out of her dress.

"You must have lain right on the bridge, dear.

There's paint everywhere," Mrs. Cobb said as she scrubbed. It was coming out, though, and that made Rebecca feel better.

"Do you have a piece of paper, Uncle Jeremiah?" she asked. "I'd like to copy out my new poem."

When she was done, she read it out loud to the Cobbs, who enjoyed it immensely.

"How in the world do you do it?" Mr. Cobb exclaimed.

"Oh, it's easy." Rebecca replied. "I love words and how they sound together. It all just comes into my head."

Mrs. Cobb smiled and asked if they could have a copy of the poem for their family Bible.

"Yes! Indeed," Rebecca said. "I'll do a pretty version with violet ink and a fine pen. But now I must see how my dress is doing."

The elderly couple followed Rebecca into the

kitchen. The dress was dry, but ruined. The colors had run with all the washing and the paint had stained. Mrs. Cobb ironed it out and Rebecca put it back on. The spots still showed, and Rebecca was very sad.

"I must get home," she said as she took her hat off the nail by the door. "If I'm going to get in trouble, I'd like it to be over quickly."

And there was a considerable amount of trouble when she got home. Aunt Miranda was upset about the ruined dress and told the girl that she could not go to Alice Robinson's birthday party. Rebecca was a brave girl and listened to her aunt with respect.

Once she was upstairs in her room, Rebecca thought of ways to teach herself a lesson for being so careless. She decided that she must give something up. She looked around her room, trying to figure out what to pick. Finally her eyes fell upon her precious parasol. That was it! But what should she do now?

She couldn't hide it in the attic, for she knew she would climb upstairs to rescue it in a moment of weakness. She looked out her window at the apple trees and thought for a moment about putting her parasol up in one. But that would be too dangerous. Her eyes looked around the yard and stopped on the well. That would do. She would fling her dearest possession down into the water!

Rebecca slowly and quietly made her way downstairs. Once outside by the well, she looked down into the darkness and bravely threw her parasol inside.

There, she thought. *I shall be a much better girl for it.*

The next morning, Rebecca woke up with a light heart and went off to school. What she didn't know was that there was some trouble with the well. When Miranda had difficulty drawing water, she called a friend to help. He lifted up the well cover and saw the trouble. The ivory hook of the parasol had caught in the gear, stopping it in its tracks. The parasol had opened up, gotten tangled in some roots, and jammed up the works. It took quite an effort to get it out!

When Rebecca got home from school that afternoon, she ended up in even more trouble. But when Aunt Miranda heard that she was simply trying to be a better girl, she said, "If you think we haven't punished you enough, you just let me know and I'll think of something else. There's no sense in punishing the whole family by making us drink ivory dust from broken parasols."

CHAPTER 9

Snow-White, Rose-Red, and Mr. Aladdin

The summer passed quickly and the seasons changed. November brought with it dull and dreary weather. There was a chill in the air, and the days were gloomy. Thanksgiving was coming. Golden pumpkins, bright yellow squash, and colorful corn were all being stored away for the season. The entire community was busy.

Clara Belle and Susan Simpson had asked Rebecca and Emma Jane for their help. The girls had been selling soap to their friends and neighbors. The Excelsior Soap Company paid little bonuses for the sale of a certain number of cakes, and the Simpsons had their hearts set on selling enough to earn a lamp.

One weekend just before Thanksgiving, Rebecca's aunts went to visit an old friend in Portland. She was spending the weekend with Emma Jane. Now that the girls were twelve, they were old enough to take a short trip on their own. The girls made plans to visit with Emma Jane's cousins in North Riverboro on Saturday. Mrs. Perkins had kindly allowed them to sell the soap to a few houses on the way there and back.

The girls woke up happy and excited on Saturday morning. They had already packed their soap into the back of the wagon. The weather was glorious and sunny. The leaves on the trees were all kinds of amazing colors—

bronze, rust, scarlet, and tawny. The air was crisp. The old horse pulling the wagon forgot his age and trotted like a colt.

As the girls carried on toward North Riverboro, they stopped off at different houses to sell the soap. One girl would hold the horse while the other would go to the door. Rebecca was very successful and had already sold three whole boxes. Emma Jane wasn't as lucky. She had only sold three single cakes. At one house a lady had put her head out the window and yelled, "Go away, little girl! Whatever you have in your box, we don't want any."

The girls pulled up to a gate with a long path leading up to the house. "It's your turn, Rebecca," Emma Jane said. "And I'm glad, too! I'm still shaking from the last house. I don't know who lives here, but the blinds are all shut. It doesn't count if there's no one home. You'll have to take the next house, too!"

Rebecca walked up the lane and went to the side door. A young man was husking corn on the porch. She was surprised to see someone sitting there, so she asked shyly, "Is the lady of the house at home?"

"I am the lady of the house this morning," the young man said and smiled. "What can I do for you?"

He was very handsome and looked to be in his early twenties. Rebecca felt shy for an instant. Then she gathered up her courage and said, "Have you ever heard of the—would you like, um—do you need any soap?"

"Do I look like I need soap?" the young man asked.

Rebecca blushed. "I didn't mean it that way! I have soap to sell." She reached into her jacket pocket and pulled out her leaflet. Then she flew into her sales pitch, just as she and Emma Jane had rehearsed.

Rebecca's new friend invited her to sit on the porch with him as they discussed the greatness of the Snow-White and Rose-Red soaps.

"I'm watching the house today for my aunt. She's gone to Portland. I used to live here with her when I was a boy. This farm is my favorite place on Earth!"

"Oh, I understand! There's a special place in the heart for the farm where one grew up," Rebecca said.

The young man put down his cob of corn. "So you think your childhood is over now, young lady?"

"I can still remember it," Rebecca said seriously. "But it seems like a very long time ago."

"Me too, and it wasn't the happiest of times," he said.

"Neither was mine." Rebecca sighed.

The two chatted like old friends. Rebecca told him all about Sunnybrook Farm, her many brothers and sisters, and about never having enough books to read. The kind stranger told her that he had never had enough food or clothes.

"But you're well now?" she asked.

"I'm doing quite well, thank you," he replied. "Now tell me, how much soap should I buy today?"

"That's a good question. Does your aunt have any at home? How much do you think she needs?" Rebecca asked.

"Oh, I'm not sure. But soap doesn't go bad, does it?" he said.

"Let me check," Rebecca replied. She pulled out the pamphlet and read more about the soap. "No, it doesn't. It holds up very well."

"Wonderful!" he said. "Now tell me, what brings you to selling soap?"

Rebecca told him all about the Simpsons and how hard they were working to earn the special lamp. In fact, she told him so much about the poor Simpsons that the young man made up his mind in an instant.

"I see," he said. "I'll take three hundred cakes. That should get them the lamp."

Rebecca was sitting on a stool very close to the edge of the porch. When she heard him say "three hundred," she was so shocked that she fell right off her stool and into the lilac bushes. Thankfully, the porch wasn't too far off the ground!

The kind young man helped her up and brushed her off. Rebecca turned bright red as she blushed.

"Are you quite sure?" Rebecca asked. "That's a lot of cakes."

"I'm absolutely sure," he replied. "What's your name, by the way?"

"Rebecca Rowena Randall, sir."

"Lovely name, indeed. Would you like to know mine?" he asked.

"I think I know already!" she exclaimed. "It's Mr. Aladdin, just like in the story about the magic lamp."

Her new friend laughed. "Well, now that you've sold all your soap, the Simpsons will surely have their lamp by Thanksgiving. In fact, I'll promise you that it will arrive in time."

Rebecca continued, "Oh please, may I run down and tell Emma Jane the good news? She'll be so happy that we've finished selling the soap!"

Mr. Aladdin nodded, and Rebecca sped off down the lane. As she got close to the wagon, she cried out, "Emma Jane! Emma Jane! We're sold out!"

"Whatever do you mean?" Emma Jane said. "That's impossible!"

"Not impossible!" Mr. Aladdin said as he approached. "I've bought three hundred cakes." He took all of the boxes out of the wagon and promised to write to the soap company about the lamp for the Simpsons that very evening.

Rebecca climbed back up into the wagon. Mr. Aladdin wrapped the blanket over both girls and said his good-byes.

"Good-bye, Mr. Aladdin!" Rebecca called back as they rode off.

Emma Jane carried on for a bit about how wonderful it was that the young man had bought all their soap and put the blanket around their knees. Then she asked if Rebecca knew his name.

"I forgot to ask properly!" she exclaimed. "I called him Mr. Aladdin because he was helping the Simpsons get their lamp."

"Oh, Rebecca!" Emma Jane said. "How could you call a perfect stranger by a nickname the first time you met him?"

"Well, it's not a nickname exactly. And he did laugh."

Just before they got to Riverboro, each girl

made a solemn promise to keep the lamp a secret. They both agreed it would be a wonderful surprise for the Simpsons on Thanksgiving. It took every effort for these two honest girls to keep the secret, but they managed.

CHAPTER 10

The Wonderful Lamp

ᢍ

The lamp arrived at the Simpsons' house on Thanksgiving Day, just as Mr. Aladdin promised it would. Seesaw Simpson took it out of the large packing crate himself and set it up in the living room. The whole family gathered around to see the lamp.

Over at the old brick house, Thanksgiving dinner had just finished. As they had for the past twenty-five years, Miranda and Jane had invited Mr. and Mrs. Cobb to celebrate the holiday with them. With the dinner dishes washed, Rebecca sat with a book and tried to read. More than anything else, she wanted to go see the Simpsons' lamp. The idea of it lighting up their house with all its glory sparkled in her imagination.

It was nearly five o'clock when she finally asked her Aunt Miranda if she could go to the Simpsons' house.

"Why do you want to run around with those Simpson children on Thanksgiving Day?" Miranda asked. "For once it might be a good idea to just sit still."

"The Simpsons have a new lamp, and Emma Jane and I promised to go see it. We thought we'd make it a party," Rebecca replied.

"Where did they get a brand-new lamp?"

"They got it as a prize for selling soap," Rebecca answered. "They've been working hard all year. Remember, Emma Jane and I helped them the weekend that you and Aunt Jane were in Portland."

"I don't remember, but that's fine. I guess you can go for an hour. Just be careful. It gets mighty dark by six o'clock this time of year." Miranda looked closely at Rebecca. "What's that making your pocket sag?"

"It's my nuts and raisins from dinner," Rebecca replied.

"Why didn't you eat them?"

"Because I was full and thought they would be good for the party," Rebecca said softly. She hated being scolded in front of company, especially Mr. and Mrs. Cobb.

Aunt Jane said quickly, "They were your own, Rebecca. If you want to save them to share with your friends, that's just fine. It is Thanksgiving, after all."

Rebecca smiled and thanked her aunts before running off to call on Emma Jane. Mr. and Mrs. Cobb gave her a warm hug before she left. They said that they had never seen a girl improve so fast in such a short period of time.

"There's plenty of room left for improvement," Aunt Miranda said. "She's always falling into mischief. Of all the foolish things—selling soap for lamps!"

"Well, the Simpsons must have done a good job of it," Mrs. Cobb said. "Adam Ladd from North Riverboro said that the girl who sold him the soap was charming and quite remarkable."

"It must have been Clara Belle Simpson. Although I'd never call her remarkable," Miranda replied. "Is Adam at home again?"

"Yes," Mrs. Cobb replied. "He's been staying with his aunt. She told me that Adam was so impressed with the girl who sold him the soap that he's planning on bringing her a Christmas present! Apparently he was completely taken by the child's dark hair and eyes," Mrs. Cobb said.

"Well, that's strange," Miranda said. "Especially considering that Clara Belle has crossed eyes and red hair."

Jane changed the subject then and asked after the Cobbs' own farm. She knew almost immediately that Mr. Ladd must have met Rebecca. Who else had brilliant eyes and a remarkable way about her?

Meanwhile, Rebecca met Emma Jane at the corner. They hugged each other quickly and started off toward the Simpsons'.

"I've got terrible news!" Emma Jane whispered.

"No! Oh no!" Rebecca cried. "Please don't tell me the lamp broke on the way there!"

"It's not broken," Emma Jane said. "It's that the Simpsons have no wicks and no lamp oil. My mother's given me some oil, but Seesaw had to go down to the neighbor's house to see if he could borrow a wick."

"Well, let's not worry about how they'll keep the lamp lit right now. I've got nuts, berries, and apples for the party," Rebecca said.

"Yes, and I've got peppermints and maple sugar," Emma Jane added. "The Simpsons finally had a real Thanksgiving dinner tonight. The doctor gave them sweet potatoes and cranberries and turnips. Father sent them some spareribs, and Mrs. Cobb gave them a chicken and some mincemeat."

The two girls knocked quietly at the door. Seesaw let them in, and they saw the lamp at once. It was beautiful! Rebecca gasped and said, "It's perfect!"

The party was great fun. The lamp stood on its table in the corner looking glorious. Each child took a turn standing in front of it. The brass shone like gold. The crimson paper glowed like a ruby. They were all just so thrilled. Emma Jane held tightly to Rebecca's hand. Soon it came time to leave. Rebecca had to drag herself away.

"I'll turn the lamp off the minute I think you're home," Clara Belle promised. "I wonder how long it will burn with the small bit of oil we have."

At that moment Seesaw came into the room and said, "You needn't worry about having no oil. There's a great keg of it out by the shed. Someone from North Riverboro sent it."

Rebecca squeezed Emma Jane's hand tightly. "I'll bet it was Mr. Aladdin!" she whispered.

Seesaw took the girls out to the gate and asked if he could walk them home. Rebecca and Emma Jane thanked him but said they'd be fine on their own.

As usual, the girls parted at the crossroads. When Rebecca got home, she found her aunts knitting in the living room. She quickly told them that the party was wonderful.

"Aunt Jane! Aunt Miranda! If you come to the

window you can see the lamp shining all red at the Simpsons' house."

"It'll probably set that house right on fire," Aunt Miranda said.

Jane went to the window to look at the lamp with Rebecca. She wanted to ask her niece about who had really sold the three hundred cakes of soap.

"Rebecca, who was it that sold the soap to Mr. Ladd in North Riverboro? Was it the Simpson sisters or was it you?"

"Mr. who?" Rebecca asked.

"Mr. Ladd, in North Riverboro."

"Is that his real name?" she asked. Laughing to herself, she said quietly, "I didn't make such a bad guess then!"

"Rebecca," Aunt Jane said sternly. "I asked who sold the soap to Adam Ladd."

"Adam Ladd!" The girl giggled again. "He's A. Ladd, too, what fun!"

"Rebecca!"

"I'm sorry, Aunt Jane. Emma Jane and I sold the soap to Mr. Ladd."

"Did you tease him or make him buy all that soap?"

"Now, Aunt Jane, how could I make a grown-up buy all that soap if he didn't want to? He said it was a present for his aunt."

Jane didn't quite know what to say. She looked at Rebecca and saw her hair falling out of its braids and her eyes sparkling. Her niece was sensitive and sweet as a rose, but as strong as an oak tree at the same time.

"Rebecca," she said with a sigh, "you look like you've got the energy of that lamp burning inside you. I wish you could take things easier. I do worry."

Rebecca nodded. The two stood at the window for a long time after that and watched the faint light in the distance.

CHAPTER 11

A Christmas Surprise

༄

Christmas Day arrived, and with it a fresh morning. Icicles hung like dazzling pendants, and white snow covered everything like a blanket. Just after breakfast, a young boy knocked at the door. When Rebecca opened it, he said, "Does Miss Rebecca Randall live here?"

She nodded, and he handed her a package. She held it lightly and carried it into the living room.

"It's a present," she said to her aunts. "It must be. Who could it be from?"

"A good way to find out would be to open it,"
Aunt Miranda said.

The package had two smaller boxes inside.
Rebecca opened them with trembling fingers.
The first had a long chain of delicate pink coral
beads. A card said, "Merry Christmas from Mr.
Aladdin." The second package contained a silver
chain with a blue locket for Emma Jane.

"Of all things!" Aunt Jane exclaimed.

"Who sent it?" Aunt Miranda asked.

"Mr. Ladd," Rebecca whispered.

"Well, I never!" Aunt Jane
said. "Mrs. Cobb mentioned
he was going to
send a present
to the girl who
sold him the
soap, but I didn't
think he actually
would."

There was another note inside saying that Mr. Ladd was coming by that afternoon to take Emma Jane and Rebecca for a ride in his new sleigh. It was to be his Christmas treat.

"How nice of him!" Aunt Jane said. "Let's finish up our breakfast, Rebecca. Then you can run over and give Emma Jane her present." She looked at her niece. "What's the matter, child?"

Rebecca was just too happy for words. A single tear fell down her cheek.

As promised, Mr. Ladd called on the girls that afternoon. They went off on a grand sleigh ride, with Rebecca and Emma Jane chattering away like happy little birds. For many nights following that wonderful day, Rebecca slept with one hand on her coral chain to make sure it was safe.

CHAPTER 12

Rebecca Represents the Family

⤜꙰⤛

In the two years that followed that wonderful Christmas, many things changed around the old brick house and around Riverboro. The Simpsons moved away, taking Seesaw, Clara Belle, and Susan with them. It was during this time that Reverend Amos Burch and his wife returned to Riverboro. They had been working abroad as preachers.

The church's Aid Society had called its meeting for a Wednesday in March. There was snow on the ground, and the sky was dark. Miranda and

Jane both had colds and were too sick to go to the meeting.

"You'll have to go for us, Rebecca. You can represent the family," Miranda said. "Reverend Burch used to know your grandfather Sawyer, so he'll be expecting us there. Be careful how you behave. Be respectful. Be sure to tell everyone what terrible colds Jane and I have."

Rebecca nodded. She was excited to go to the society meeting and represent the family. Aunt Jane wrote her a note explaining why she had to miss school and sent her off.

The service was held in the Sunday school room. Reverend Burch was at the front of the room about to begin by the time Rebecca arrived. There were a dozen people at the meeting. Being the youngest one there, Rebecca found a friendly face in Mrs. Cobb and sat down beside her.

"Both of my aunts have bad colds," she said to her friend, "so they've sent me instead."

Mrs. Cobb smiled and patted Rebecca on the knee. Mrs. Burch was sitting on her other side. She was a slim woman with dark hair and a broad forehead. She was wearing a well-worn black silk dress and looked very tired. Rebecca's heart went out to her.

The meeting began with a prayer. Then Reverend Burch asked if someone would play the piano.

"Oh, Rebecca, why don't you!" Mrs. Cobb said.

Rebecca went to the front of the room and sat down behind the instrument. Her father had taught her to play the piano when she was very small, but she didn't get the chance to do it very often. She played a few hymns while the group sang along.

After she played the last hymn, Reverend Burch told everyone that he and his wife would be in town for the evening. He said that he would love to hold a parlor meeting and asked if anyone would be willing to host their family.

No one said a word. Some of the ladies had no spare room. Some had sickness in the family. Mrs. Burch sat there with her hands wound tightly together.

Why won't anyone speak? Rebecca thought. Her heart fluttered with sympathy. Mrs. Cobb whispered, "Your grandfather always used to entertain missionaries at the brick house, Rebecca. He'd never let them sleep anywhere else while he was alive."

Rebecca thought Mrs. Cobb was telling her to invite them to stay, so she gathered up her courage and rose from her seat.

"My aunts, Miranda and Jane, would be very happy to have you visit them at the brick house."

Reverend Burch smiled kindly and said that he would be delighted. They spent the rest of the afternoon on the Aid Society's business. Much to her surprise, the reverend asked Rebecca to lead the final prayer!

She stood up, a bit shaky at first, and began slowly. Out came a strange mixture of every hymn, prayer, and speech she had ever heard. After the breathless "Amen," she sat back down, grateful for her chair. It took quite some time for her knees to stop shaking.

Mrs. Burch came up to Rebecca afterward and said, "My dear! I am so glad we'll be staying with you. Would it be all right if we came at half past five? It's three now, and we need to get the children and our bags."

Rebecca told her that half past five was the time they usually had dinner, so that would be a fine time for them to arrive.

"Wonderful!" Mrs. Burch said. "I look forward to seeing you again."

Mrs. Cobb came up and offered to drive
Rebecca home. Suddenly the full weight of having invited the Burches as company before asking
her aunts settled on her shoulders. The drive
home was very quiet. But by the time she arrived
back at the brick house, Rebecca had become very
excited about the whole idea—despite what Aunt
Miranda might say!

⁓

Rebecca took off her shoes and put on her slippers
before entering the parlor where her aunts where
knitting.

"It was a very small meeting, Aunt Miranda,"
she said slowly. "The reverend and his wife are
lovely people. They're coming here to spend
tonight and tomorrow with you. I hope you
won't mind."

"Coming here!" Miranda cried. Her knitting
fell into her lap. "Did they invite themselves?"

"No," Rebecca answered truthfully. "I had to invite them for you, like when Grandfather was alive."

"When are they coming? Right away?"

"No, not for two hours—about half past five."

Miranda was very upset. They had had no company at the brick house for many years. Now in a mere two hours it would be full of strangers!

"How in the world did you let this happen, Rebecca? What were you—"

"Now, Miranda," Jane interrupted. "I thought this might come up. You know how much our father enjoyed helping the preachers."

Rebecca told them about playing the piano for the Reverend Burch. She told them all that had happened at the meeting and brought home all the news about the Aid Society. She let her aunts know how hard it was to sit there with no one to offer the kind people a place to stay. Then she told them how Mrs. Cobb said that her grandfather always used to have them at the brick house. She felt she just had to speak up.

"Reverend Burch said a prayer for Grandfather right then and there. He spoke about what a wonderful man he was, and I knew I must have done the right thing, Aunt Miranda."

At that, Aunt Miranda's heart softened. The memories of the old days came flooding over her. She thought about her father. He was such a good man. The old brick house had always been full of interesting people coming and going from faraway places.

"You've only done what's polite. It's just too bad that Jane and I are sick with colds. That just goes to show that it's right as rain to keep your house clean and shiny, with company stopping by at a moment's notice."

Rebecca kindly offered to get the rooms ready for the guests while her aunts had a good rest. What good work she did! She tidied the rooms, placed fresh towels on the washstands, and made the beds with fresh linens. Rebecca even opened up the good parlor, lit a fresh fire, and turned on her own lamp. The lamp was another Christmas present from Mr. Aladdin. He sent them every year.

By a quarter after five, everything was ready. The Burch family arrived promptly at five thirty. Rebecca played with the two small girls until dinner while Aunt Jane spoke with the reverend and his wife.

Aunt Miranda made a grand meal. Mr. and Mrs. Cobb joined them, too. After dinner, they all told stories around the warm fire Rebecca had lit. Later, they shared cookies and raspberry lemonade, and then Rebecca took the young girls off to bed. Mr. and Mrs. Cobb also said good night.

"Your niece is quite remarkable!" Reverend Burch said to Miranda.

"She seems to be turning out well, indeed.

She was quite a handful when she first arrived."

"Do you know who she reminds me of, Miranda?" Reverend Burch said. "Her grandfather—she's the spitting image of her father on the outside, but she's all Sawyer on the inside, I believe."

"Well," Miranda replied. "We'll just have to see about that, won't we."

᠊ᢏᡂᢇ᠊

The next morning Rebecca woke up earlier than usual. She jumped out of bed and quickly got dressed.

I know my aunts are still feeling poorly, she thought. *I'll go and get breakfast started.*

Jane's cold had grown worse overnight, and she was unable to get out of bed. Miranda was still under the weather, but she managed to get up anyway—although she complained about having all the guests in the house.

By the time she got downstairs, she discovered that Rebecca had already done everything! The coffee was made, the eggs were cooking, and the fires were lit. Miranda looked around the room with an honest sense of pride at her niece's hard work. The Burch family enjoyed their second meal with Rebecca and her aunts. They were all very sad when they had to leave. The two little girls cried and cried. Then they made Rebecca promise to write often.

Reverend and Mrs. Burch thanked the Sawyers for their kindness and said that they would always remember the lovely time they had there. Those two days became fond memories for everyone, but especially for Rebecca.

CHAPTER 13

Days at a New School

⁓

Now that Rebecca was too old to go to the little schoolhouse, her aunts sent her to a boarding school in the town of Wareham. It was an excellent school, and she was very lucky to be going there. During the summer, Rebecca and Emma Jane took the train to school every day. They often shared a ride with Huldah Meserve, who also lived in Riverboro. In the winter months, they boarded with the rest of the students.

Rebecca's favorite class was English literature

and composition. It was taught by Miss Emily Maxwell, a young teacher who was also a published writer. One day Miss Maxwell asked the class to bring in a piece of writing from the year before. She wanted to see how they had all improved.

All of Rebecca's work was packed away in the attic of the old brick house. But she did have her book of poetry, which she shyly handed over to her teacher.

"I know it's not very good, Miss Maxwell," she said. "I hope you can help me get better."

The teacher took the book Rebecca had in her hands. "I promise I'll read it over with a careful eye."

The book appeared on Miss Maxwell's desk three days later. Rebecca knew that her teacher had read her poetry and was going to talk to her about it. Her stomach was full of butterflies!

"Did you think these were very good?" Miss Maxwell asked after all the other students had left.

"Not very," Rebecca said honestly. "My neighbors the Cobbs always liked them, but it's hard to tell when you're the one writing them. Mrs. Perkins once told me they were better than Longfellow, but I knew that couldn't be true."

Miss Maxwell smiled kindly. "I'm afraid your first instincts were correct. They do need some work."

"Then I must give up all hope of ever being a writer!" Rebecca replied with a sigh.

"Not so fast!" Miss Maxwell said. "They do show promise. You have a great imagination, Rebecca. You just need more practice."

The two sat in the classroom and talked for a while about how Rebecca could become a better writer. Miss Maxwell told her to write all the time. She said that was the only way for her to

truly improve. Rebecca came away from that class with a lot of extra homework, but she didn't mind. She was so inspired by Miss Maxwell and her good advice.

CHAPTER 14

A Visit from Mr. Aladdin

~

The warm months passed and soon it was time for Rebecca and Emma Jane to stay at school. The first winter Rebecca spent at Wareham as a boarding student was one of the happiest of her life. She and Emma Jane were roommates. They had arrived at school just after Christmas, during the coldest months of the year. They brought all kinds of presents with them and had just finished setting up their room when Huldah knocked on the door.

"Why, don't you girls have a lovely room here!" she said as she came inside. "Look at that wonderful screen!"

"Oh, the screen was a present from Mr. Ladd," Emma Jane said.

"It's so stylish! You two were lucky when you met him. And to think, he's kept in touch with you all these years." Huldah sat down on a chair just inside the room. She was a pretty girl with lovely red hair. But she was also vain and spent far too much time thinking about her appearance.

"Isn't this your study hour?" Emma Jane asked.

Huldah said that indeed it was, but she had lost her Latin grammar book in the hallway yesterday and was waiting for a young man to return it.

"I do have another book that Mr. Morrison said I could use while I wait for mine to be returned," Huldah continued. "There was a perfectly elegant gentleman in his office when I went to ask about my book. He was so handsome! He looked at me the entire time I was in there."

"You'll have to wear a mask if you're to get any work done at all, Huldah," Rebecca said dryly.

"You know, he had a perfectly gorgeous ring, too," Huldah continued dreamily. "It sparkled and wound around and around his finger. I've never seen anything like it." Just then the bell rang. "Oh dear, I must run! Where has the hour gone?"

Rebecca knew that it was probably Mr. Aladdin in the office. He was a trustee of the school, and she remembered that he had just such a ring.

After Huldah left, Rebecca went out on her own to see Miss Maxwell. She often spent Fridays reading at her teacher's house. It was her favorite time of the week. She pulled *David Copperfield* down from the shelves and fell into a chair. She read for half an hour before looking out the window.

There, coming down the path, were Mr. Aladdin and Huldah! Rebecca didn't know what to think except that she didn't want to share her friend with Huldah. She sat back down in the chair and closed her book tightly. *She must have walked him over here on her way to class*, Rebecca thought. She was very happy when Mr. Ladd reached the front gate of the house and said goodbye to Huldah.

Suddenly the door opened and someone called out, "Hello? Miss Maxwell said that I could find Rebecca Rowena Randall here?"

Rebecca jumped to her feet. "Mr. Aladdin! Oh, I knew you were in Wareham, but I was afraid you wouldn't have time to come see me."

"Now, now," Mr. Ladd said. "I always have time for a visit with you!"

The two sat down and had a merry conversation. Rebecca was saddened when he got up to go, but he promised to return soon.

"Enjoy your time at school, Rebecca," he said kindly. "It's meant to be the best of your life."

"I promise!" She smiled up at his handsome face. "I cross my heart and promise!"

CHAPTER 15

Illness, Schoolwork, and Mr. Aladdin's Visit

∽

The first happy year at Wareham was over and gone. September had come, and Rebecca was back in school. She had spent most of the summer studying. That fall, she became the assistant editor of the *Wareham School Pilot*. She was the first girl to hold the post at the school newspaper. It was her greatest triumph.

Although Rebecca worked hard, she was far from the best student. Many of the girls were better at math and science. But Rebecca had a natural curiosity and a love of school that made her continue to try. As rewarding as life at school was, life at the old brick house was equally hard.

"Aunt Jane," Rebecca said one afternoon, "it seems like nothing I do suits Aunt Miranda these days." Her eyes filled with tears.

Rebecca's tears brought tears to Jane's eyes as she comforted her niece. "You must be patient." She wiped her tears and then Rebecca's. "I didn't tell you because I didn't want you to worry, but Aunt Miranda isn't well. There are other problems, too, things you needn't be concerned about. Just try to be kind to her, even if it's hard. She's been so proud of you lately."

"Oh, the poor dear! Don't worry, Aunt Jane. I'll put my best face forward."

When Rebecca carried up some toast for her aunt later in the day, that's exactly what she did. She used the best china plates and brought her a pretty flower, too.

"Now, Aunt Miranda, I know you don't want

me to make a fuss, but I thought some toast would make you feel better," Rebecca said cheerfully.

"Thank you, Rebecca. It looks good. But you shouldn't have wasted a perfectly good flower," Miranda said.

"You can't say that it's a waste if it brightens up your day just a bit!" Rebecca replied.

Miranda put her best face forward, too. She was under the weather, that was true, but there was something else. Years ago, she and Jane had invested some money in a business that was no longer working. They hadn't lost a huge amount, but it came at a time when Rebecca's school fees were due.

The two aunts decided they would scrimp and save every possible penny. They had promised Rebecca's mother that they would give the girl an education, and that's just what they intended to do!

ᦥ

Rebecca and Emma Jane sat in their room talking. "If only we could be roommates forever!" Emma Jane said. "We get along so well and it would make me quite happy."

"I'd like that, too," Rebecca said, "but I've already promised to help my brother John with his housekeeping after he becomes a doctor. That's his deepest wish. We've talked about it in letter after letter."

"He won't have his own house for many years, though, will he?" Emma Jane asked.

"No." Rebecca sighed and flung herself on her bed. "Not unless we can pay off the debt on Sunnybrook Farm."

"It'll work out, Rebecca. I know it will," Emma Jane said kindly.

Rebecca turned over and said, "It's only twelve hundred dollars, but it's so much to my family. They've been working so hard, but it never seems to get any better. I'll be done with school in a year or two. At least then I can help."

"Will you be a teacher or a writer before you go to live with John?" Emma Jane asked.

"I suppose I'll do whichever comes first."

"You could go with the Burch family and do preaching work. They're always asking about you."

"No, I don't think that's for me. I don't want to go thousands of miles away from home to teach things that I'm not sure I know myself."

So Rebecca and Emma Jane sat and thought about life after school. Each girl was completely lost in her own little world.

⌒

Mr. Adam Ladd was on his way back from Temperance one afternoon when he decided to visit Rebecca at Wareham. He also had some business to discuss with the principal. It was the school's fiftieth anniversary, and Mr. Ladd knew he wanted to do something special for them.

But mainly he wanted to see Rebecca. He had heard about the trouble with Sunnybrook Farm and knew that Miranda was not well. He wanted to see how Rebecca was holding up.

Rebecca and Mr. Ladd walked around the woods beside the Wareham school. He took a good look at his friend and saw that she was thin and drawn. She wore an old dress of her Aunt Jane's, which was looking rather shabby. He knew that her pretty eyes and good nature would triumph over her problems, but he was still worried.

"I do think you might be studying too hard, Rebecca. You're looking quite tired," he said as they strolled along.

"Well, maybe just a little. But vacation is coming up soon," she said with a smile.

"And are you going to have a good rest? You need to recover those dimples! They're worth it," he said.

A shadow fell over Rebecca's face. She held back her tears, "Oh, Mr. Aladdin," she cried. "It's just not one of my dimple days. I am afraid my Aunt Miranda isn't well, and there's something else worrying her that she hasn't told me." Rebecca waved good-bye and ran off.

Mr. Ladd walked toward the principal's office deep in thought. He wanted to finish up his plans to contribute to the school's fiftieth anniversary. He planned to give the library a gift of books, but he also wanted to hold an essay competition. The two top essays would win a grand prize. He just didn't know yet what the prize would be.

When he finished speaking with the principal about his plans, Mr. Ladd went to speak to Miss Maxwell. He wanted to help Rebecca, but he knew she would never accept his money. *I know she'll tell me she must earn it herself, the good soul!*

Mr. Ladd had barely stepped through the door when he said, "Miss Maxwell, have you noticed that Rebecca looks so very tired these days?"

Miss Maxwell took his hat and coat and said, "Yes, indeed she does. I was thinking of taking her away with me. I always go south for the spring vacation—to Old Point Comfort. I think Rebecca would enjoy coming along."

"That's a perfect idea!" Mr. Ladd said. "Of course you'll let me help pay her way. From the very moment I met her, I knew she was an extraordinary child. She deserves some help in this world."

"I agree. She needs a dozen things money could buy. I only wish I were a rich woman," Miss Maxwell said.

"Well then, let me act through you," Mr. Ladd said. "It would be my pleasure to help. I asked Miranda to let me provide her with a musical education, but she wouldn't hear of it."

"They are proud, the Sawyer women. But the hard work and lack of money have made Rebecca who she is. She's got a great character because of it. I do think this matter should be kept between the two of us."

Mr. Ladd smiled and said, "You are a true fairy godmother." He turned and gazed out the window. "Oh look, there she is now!"

Rebecca was walking down the street with a young man her own age. She smiled up at him as they read something together. Her eyes sparkled and there was a spring in her step. Rebecca wasn't interested in dating boys, though. Not like Huldah was, anyway! She and the boy were just friends, but it caused a bit of a stir with Mr. Ladd.

"I daresay, as much as I support the Wareham

school, I'm not sure I agree with boys and girls attending classes together," Mr. Ladd said.

Miss Maxwell laughed. "I have my own doubts sometimes, but that's an impressive sight in front of you. The junior and senior editors of the *Pilot* are actually getting along with each other!"

CHAPTER 16

Roses of Joy

∼☙

The day before Rebecca was to set off on her trip with Miss Maxwell, she went to the library with Emma Jane and Huldah. They had just finished studying and were on their way out when they stopped to look at the books in the glass case by the front entrance. These shelves held the special fiction books that the students were not allowed to read while they had their studies to concentrate on.

A new book called *The Rose of Joy* caught Rebecca's eye.

"What does it mean?" she wondered out loud. The three girls stopped to talk about it for a minute. Emma Jane thought it meant success. Huldah said that her rose of joy would be spending a year in the city, dressed in the latest fashions. Rebecca announced that it must mean love. Emma Jane agreed that this was the best guess.

Rebecca and Emma Jane were still thinking about the title of the book that evening. It kept both of them up whispering well past the time they should be sleeping. They talked on and on about the possible meanings. Could it be helpfulness? Could it be doing something perfectly—like a painting or a poem?

"I think it could be any of those things," Emma Jane said sleepily before she drifted off to her dreamland. Rebecca lay awake for hours afterward wondering what the rose of joy truly was.

The next morning she left for her vacation. It

was all so inspiring! The ocean and the strange new sights worked their magic. Within three days, Rebecca felt much better. She and Miss Maxwell had wonderful talks and spent hours walking by the water. The two got along very well.

During this time, Rebecca thought a lot about Mr. Ladd's essay competition. She wanted to win, if only to prove that she was worthy of his friendship.

"I'd like to talk to you about the topics I've been thinking about," Rebecca said to Miss Maxwell. "That way you can tell me which one you think I could write the best."

"The subject is important," Miss Maxwell said. "I dare not choose one for you."

"But I think of a new one every night! I don't know how to pick."

"You need to just choose one and get started. I find that's always the best way."

"Have you ever heard of *The Rose of Joy*?" Rebecca asked.

"Yes, of course. Where did you see that?"

"I saw it in the library the day before we left. Do you know what it means?"

"I'm afraid it's very hard to explain."

"Oh, please try, Miss Maxwell. I've been thinking about it for so long."

Miss Maxwell told Rebecca that the poem dealt with themes of sorrow and joy. She said that the title came from a line in the verse. Rebecca listened closely to what her teacher said.

"That's it!" Rebecca exclaimed. "That's what I'll write my essay about! I'm going to write about my very own Rose of Joy."

And write it she did. Rebecca's essay won the girl's prize, and with it, a hard-earned fifty dollars, which she sent home to help with the mortgage. There was even a ceremony at the school where Rebecca shook the governor's hand! Her aunts, the Cobbs, and many other friends and family were in the audience to see her moment of glory. She was nervous standing in front of all the people, but she was also very proud. She had worked hard and absolutely deserved to win.

CHAPTER 17

The Vision Splendid

⌒

In the year after Rebecca won the essay contest, Huldah graduated from school. Now it was just Emma Jane and Rebecca who took the train during the warmer months and boarded in the winter. Rebecca was extremely busy with her studies. She expected to graduate at the end of this school year. Her days at her aunts' house were often filled with hard work as well. Rebecca did her very best to help them wherever she could. Her Aunt Miranda's health had improved, and the two were getting along better than they ever had. The days flew by.

Soon classes were finished and she was all set to graduate from the Wareham school. On the day of her graduation, Rebecca woke, jumped out of bed, and looked out the window. The sun was shining brightly in the sky.

Emma Jane opened her eyes and said, "Oh, it's a beautiful day. I'm so happy the weather is good!"

Rebecca laughed. "I'm thankful, too. Now if only I could get the class poem out of my head to make room for everything else I have to remember for today!"

The excitement felt in their little room echoed all across town. Mothers and fathers of the students had been arriving for a week. The town was bustling with the events of the day. The streets were filled with people wearing their best clothes. The girls had been making Rebecca's dress for weeks. They had only just finished it the night before.

That morning, the two girls dressed in their room for the last time. Emma Jane was going to miss Rebecca, who had been offered two different teaching positions. One was as an assistant to a music teacher at another boarding school. The other was as an assistant at the Edgewood high school. Miss Maxwell thought the second job would be better, as it would further Rebecca's own education. She would be able to take classes at the local college.

"Emma," Rebecca said as she looked at her friend, "don't you dare cry! I'm about to cry myself."

She hugged her friend and said, "I must go now or else I'll miss the coach taking us all to the ceremony."

Rebecca sat high in the coach as the horses trotted along. She saw Mr. Ladd and waved. He waved back. As he walked toward the school for the ceremony, he heard a tiny sob behind him.

"Why, Emma Jane, is that you? What's wrong?" he asked kindly.

"Oh, Mr. Ladd! Rebecca made me promise not to cry in front of her, but now that she's gone off I just had to. She's leaving a year early, and I know she worked so hard to do that, but I'm going to miss her so much!"

The pair walked toward the old meeting-house where the ceremony was to be held. The inside was decorated with white, green, and yellow ribbons.

When Rebecca looked out into the audience, she saw her sister Hannah and her brother John. Her mother had stayed behind at Sunnybrook Farm to watch her other siblings. There was no money for a new dress, anyway. The Cobbs were there as well. Mr. Cobb was beaming with pride. Rebecca knew Aunt Miranda couldn't come because her health was still too fragile, but she was surprised when she couldn't find Aunt Jane.

Rebecca sang at the top of her voice with the other students. They sang their class song and the school's anthem. The speeches went off without a hitch. Even Rebecca's class poem went over well. And then it was all over. Each girl went forward to bow and receive her diploma.

Afterward, Rebecca found Mr. Ladd. He was smiling at her. "Are you proud, sir?" she asked him.

He looked at her and said, "The proudest I've been in my life!"

Just then Mr. and Mrs. Cobb came over. She introduced them to Mr. Ladd and asked, "Where is Aunt Jane?"

"I'm sorry, young miss," Mr. Cobb said. "We've got some sad news for you."

"Is Aunt Miranda worse?" She looked at them. "Oh, she is, I can see it in your eyes!"

"She had a stroke, deary—yesterday morning. Jane said we weren't to tell you until the ceremony was all over and done with," Mrs. Cobb said.

"I'll go right home with you both," Rebecca said. "Poor Aunt Miranda—to think of how poorly she must feel, and I've been so happy all day long."

"Now, now," Mrs. Cobb said. "Your aunt said that she's doing much better. Jane made us promise that you'd not rush home."

Mr. Ladd said, "I'll take you home tomorrow, Rebecca, if that's all right with the Cobbs."

"Thank you, Mr. Ladd. Thank you!" Rebecca said.

～

Rebecca had been home at the old brick house for several days before Aunt Miranda asked for her.

When she finally went upstairs, she was shocked at how sickly her aunt looked. Her thin body looked frail under the sheets.

"Come right in, child," Aunt Miranda said, "I'm not dead yet!"

Rebecca stepped into the room and tried not to cry. They spoke about her graduation and about Sunnybrook Farm. In her own way, Aunt Miranda told Rebecca that she was very proud of her for finishing school. And Rebecca, in her own way, told

her aunt how thankful she was for all that she had given her.

Rebecca stayed by her aunt's side, holding her hand, until the sun went down. Then she and her aunts shared supper together one last time. It was a quiet, peaceful evening.

When Jane and Rebecca woke the next morning, they found that Miranda had passed away in her sleep. They wept together and knew they would miss her terribly.

"Now, Rebecca," Aunt Jane asked, "you aren't still upset with her about how she raised you, are you?"

"Oh, Aunt Jane," Rebecca replied, "of course not. Being here with the two of you made me who I am, and I'm proud of that. Very proud."

Coming to the old brick house had certainly been the making of Rebecca. The death of a loved one is so bittersweet, especially when one learns of their kindnesses. For Miranda had willed the old brick house to Rebecca. She and Jane had made plans for Rebecca's family to come and live there once they could sell Sunnybrook Farm— and finally pay off their mortgage!

Life begins again, with a whole new family to grow up within the walls of the great house. And Rebecca? Her own future was close at hand. She had so many possibilities, good friends, and the support of her dear Mr. Aladdin. She leaned her head against the door and looked out across the lands. Then she said, "Bless the brick house! Bless Aunt Miranda! Bless everything that is to be!"

What Do *You* Think?
Questions for Discussion

ⴲ

Have you ever been around a toddler who keeps asking the question "Why?" Does your teacher call on you in class with questions from your homework? Do your parents ask you questions about your day at the dinner table? We are always surrounded by questions that need a specific response. But is it possible to have a question with no right answer?

The following questions are about the book

you just read. But this is not a quiz! They are designed to help you look at the people, places, and events in the story from different angles. These questions do not have specific answers. Instead, they might make you think of the story in a completely new way.

Think carefully about each question and enjoy discovering more about this classic story.

1. Why do you think Rebecca is so excited about leaving her mother? Have you ever gone on a trip? Where did you go?

2. Mr. Cobb says that Rebecca is the oddest child he has ever met. What about Rebecca makes her strange or unusual? Have you ever met anyone like her?

3. Rebecca says of Paris, "It's the grandest place on Earth.... I can see it so clearly when I close my eyes." Do you believe that the real Paris is as beautiful as the one in her mind? What do you imagine when you close your eyes?

4. Rebecca says that she wears her dress backward to make it easier to button. Do you think this is silly or creative? Have you ever done something that other people thought was silly?

5. How is Rebecca's classroom different from school today? Do you like school? What is your favorite subject? What is your least favorite?

6. Why do you think Miranda is so against Rebecca having a pink or blue dress? Have you ever wanted something you were told you couldn't have? Did you get it?

7. Why do Rebecca's eyes well up with tears when the whole class applauds her drawing? Have you ever felt that way? What have you done that you are the most proud of?

8. Aunt Jane says of Rebecca, "I don't think she's much like the rest of us, but she's got it in her to be whatever she wants to be when she grows up." Do you agree? What do you want to do when you grow up?

9. Why do you suppose Adam Ladd buys all of Rebecca's soap? Have you ever tried to sell anything? How did it turn out?

10. What does Miss Maxwell say the Rose of Joy is? What do you think it means to Rebecca? What does it mean to you?

Afterword

by Arthur Pober, Ed.D.

❧

First impressions are important.

Whether we are meeting new people, going to new places, or picking up a book unknown to us, first impressions count for a lot. They can lead to warm, lasting memories or can make us shy away from any future encounters.

Can you recall your own first impressions and earliest memories of reading the classics?

Do you remember wading through pages and pages of text to prepare for an exam? Or were you the child who hid under the blanket to read with a flashlight, joining forces with Robin Hood to save Maid Marian? Do you remember only how long it took you to read a lengthy novel such as *Little Women*? Or did you become best friends with the March sisters?

Even for a gifted young reader, getting through long chapters with dense language can easily become overwhelming and can obscure the richness of the story and its characters. Reading an abridged, newly crafted version of a classic novel can be the gentle introduction a child needs to explore the characters and storyline without the frustration of difficult vocabulary and complex themes.

Reading an abridged version of a classic novel gives the young reader a sense of independence and the satisfaction of finishing a "grown-up" book. And when a child is engaged with and inspired by a classic story, the tone is set for further exploration of the story's themes, characters, history, and details. As a child's reading skills advance, the desire to tackle the original, unabridged version of the story will naturally emerge.

If made accessible to young readers, these stories can become invaluable tools for understanding themselves in the context of their families and social environments. This is why the Classic Starts series includes questions that stimulate discussion regarding the impact and social relevance of the characters and stories today. These questions can foster lively conversations between children and their parents or teachers. When we look at the issues, values, and standards of past times in terms of how we live now, we can appreciate literature's classic tales in a very personal and engaging way.

Share your love of reading the classics with a young child, and introduce an imaginary world real enough to last a lifetime.

Dr. Arthur Pober, Ed.D.

Dr. Arthur Pober has spent more than twenty years in the fields of early childhood and gifted education. He is the former principal of one of the world's oldest laboratory schools for gifted youngsters, Hunter College Elementary School, and former Director of Magnet Schools for the Gifted and Talented for more than 25,000 youngsters in New York City.

Dr. Pober is a recognized authority in the areas of media and child protection and is currently the U.S. representative to the European Institute for the Media and European Advertising Standards Alliance.

Explore these wonderful stories in our
Classic Starts™ library.

Oliver Twist

Pollyanna

The Prince and the Pauper

Rebecca of Sunnybrook Farm

The Red Badge of Courage

Robinson Crusoe

The Secret Garden

The Story of King Arthur and His Knights

The Strange Case of Dr. Jekyll and Mr. Hyde

The Swiss Family Robinson

The Three Musketeers

Treasure Island

The War of the Worlds

White Fang

The Wind in the Willows